LINDSAY MACRAE

You Canny Shove Yer Granny off a Bus!

Illustrated by Steven Appleby

PUFFIN BOOKS

For Charles and Kitty

PUFFIN BOOKS

Published by the Penguin Group
Penguin Books Ltd, 27 Wrights Lane, London W8 5TZ, England
Penguin Books USA Inc., 375 Hudson Street, New York, New York 10014, USA
Penguin Books Australia Ltd, Ringwood, Victoria, Australia
Penguin Books Canada Ltd, 10 Alcorn Avenue, Toronto, Ontario, Canada M4V 3B2
Penguin Books (NZ) Ltd, 182–190 Wairau Road, Auckland 10, New Zealand

Penguin Books Ltd, Registered Offices: Harmondsworth, Middlesex, England

First published by Viking 1995
Published in Puffin Books 1996
1 3 5 7 9 10 8 6 4 2

Text copyright © Lindsay MacRae, 1995
Illustrations copyright © Steven Appleby, 1995
All rights reserved

The moral right of the author has been asserted

Filmset in Baskerville

Made and printed in England by Clays Ltd, St Ives plc

Lindsay MacRae is active organizing poetry events in London and across the country, as well as being a television presenter. She has appeared on *The Children's Channel* on ITV and *Network 7* on Channel 4. This is her first solo collection, although she has contributed to other anthologies.

Contents

You Canny Shove Yer Granny off a Bus   9

Frank Doesn't Like Football (In Fact, He
   Hates It)   10

Frank the Hero   12

Frank's Dog   13

Grandad's Snoring Is Getting Boring   14

Camping with Dad (Oh, What Fun)   16

High Noon at Barking Odeon   17

Animal Rights   18

Dad Can't Dance   19

Typecasting the School Nativity Play   21

Getting Rid of My Sister   21

Playing Dead   22

The Boy Whose Imagination Ran Away
   with Him   24

Perfect Paula   25

Perfect Paula's New Year Resolutions List   26

Grubby Grimethorpe Deals with Dirt   28

Chuck-it-up Charlie   30

The Boy Who Dropped Litter   32

The Boy Who Can't Spell Tries to Look Up Rude
   Words in the Dictionary   34

Read All About It ...   34

Refugee   36

The Facts of Life   37

Just One Day   40

Whose Baby?   41

Why?   42

The Loneliness of the Long-Distance Poet   44
I'm Sorry, I've Got a Frog in My Throat   45
Plenty More Fish in the Sea   46
Derek the Hula Hula Fish   48
Cecil the Sloth   49
Vince the Confused Alsatian   50
The Boy Who Spoke Absolute Rubbish   51
Little Miss Muffet Fancies a Change   52
Little Jack Horner (Flyweight)   54
Humpty Dumpty (The True Story)   55
Mary, Mary Quite Contrary   56
Georgy Porgy Was Not Gorgy   57
Dog Poo Haiku   58
Gnu Haiku   58
Kangaroo Haiku   59
Canoe Haiku   59
Angry Loo Haiku   59
Bored to Death   60
The Fibber   62
The Boy Who Ate His Sandwiches Too Early
   While on the School Trip   64
Something's Alive in My Swimming Bag   66
Egghead   67
A Scab's Complaint   67
Rant About Pants   68
I Am a Camera   70
Mrs Wisley's Handbag   72
Mr Plunkett's Trousers   73
A Luvvy Wins an Award   74
When Anthony Wriggly Was a New Boy   75
Down with the Press   76
The Punishment   77

Children Also Get Depressed   79
2 Poems About 4 Eyes   81
Little Red Riding Hood (The Happy Version)   82
Getting Glasses When You're Older   83
The Richest Poor Man in the Valley   84
Tales Your Mother Tells You   86
RIPs (Really Implausible People)   89
Anthony Wriggly's School Report   91
The Thing About Aardvarks . . .   92

Index of First Lines   94

You Canny Shove Yer Granny off a Bus

Oh you canny
shove yer Granny
off a bus.
The authorities
will make a dreadful fuss.

(from *Trad. Scottish*)

Bravo
Crackle
Alpha...

Frank Doesn't Like Football
(In Fact, He Hates It)

It's breaktime in the playground.
The boys are picking teams.
And as long as you are not a girl,
you're in the team, it seems.

Frank wishes he was female,
a sandwich or a brick,
anything at all, so he can't play ball,
'cos football makes him sick.

But there's 9 other boys in the huddle
and nowhere he can hide.
They tell him: 'You've gotta play with us,
we're playing 5 a side.'

The goal's between 2 jumpers
and Frank is meant to save
whatever they can kick at him,
but he knows he's not that brave.

His legs turn into jelly,
his palms begin to sweat.
They aim the ball at his private parts,
it's a goal he won't forget.

The final score is 15 nil,
such a convincing win
that Frank is sure that next time out
they won't be picking him.

But the captain says to Frankie:
'You're useless, but you tried.
And to make it fair, tomorrow
you'll be on the other side.'

Frank wonders if he grows up bad
and eventually goes to Hell
that along with fire and brimstone
they play football there as well.

Frank the Hero

F – fit but not fond of football
R – rarely seen on the terraces
A – always on the losing side
N – not one to chant 'over 'ere Trevor on the 'ead'
K – keen on swimming though

T – tremendously good at the front crawl
H – head over heels underwater turns, no problem
E – even does the butterfly without goggles on

H – heroic? You bet. He saw someone drowning once
E – everyone else just stood around panicking. But Frank
R – rushed fearlessly into the muddy canal
O – only to find he'd saved a stuntman and that the panickers were in fact actors filming a TV cop show

Frank's Dog

Frank has a dog
Called John Paul Sartre
Who can't stand football either
When he tries to take him for a walk
He's not exactly eager

He doesn't get on
With other dogs
He thinks they're really thick
He'd rather have a game of chess
Than chase after a stick

He is an
Existentialdog
He lives life to the full
He doesn't get off on chocky-drops
But croissants make him drool

'Why can't you be
Like other dogs?'
Poor Frank is heard to mutter
'The huge Alsatian two doors down
Thinks you're a barking nutter.'

He is an
Intellectualdog
Who'd have won the Nobel Prize
If only he hadn't been put on earth
In doggedly disguise

Grandad's Snoring Is Getting Boring

Grandad is snoring
I can hear my
Granny screaming
SHUT UP WILL YOU!
and he will
shut up
turn over . . .

GRANNY

and start again
Grandad is snoring
it fills the dark house
like the lonely
mating call
of a lovesick
llama
Grandad is snoring
my brother
wraps his head
in the pillow
like a beefburger
in a bun
Grandad is snoring
my mother
stomps into
the bathroom
snaps on
the light
and brushes her teeth
again

BABY

DAD

ME

MUM

Good morning, everyone!

GRANDAD

Grandad is snoring
it is enough
to wake
the dead
but not enough
to wake
Grandad
and in
the morning
exhausted and
y a w n i n g
feeling more
like a lilo
with a puncture
than a
human being
I say:
Grandad
d'you know
that last night
you were snoring
and he says
perkily
Nonsense
I NEVER
SNORE
you must
have been
dreaming,

15

Camping with Dad (Oh, What Fun)

Our dad is addicted to camping
to tents which are crawling with grubs.
In our camp-beds we dream of Majorca
while he wanders off to the pub.

My mum has refused to come with us,
she's allergic to grass, trees and flowers,
though at home she puts on her bikini
and lies in the garden for hours.

Dad plays his guitar by the camp-fire
and sings very loud, out of tune.
He sounds like someone who's broken his leg
or a dog howling up at the moon.

At daybreak he wakes us with porridge,
by ten we are digging latrines,
by four we've walked miles across country
like a super-fit bunch of marines.

I wonder if dad is a sadist
who gets pleasure from torturing kids
or just caught up in some weird tradition
of doing what his father did.

High Noon at Barking Odeon

Auntie Doris and my mum
are fighting in the cinema queue.
It's a strange adult conflict
this battle of wills,
for whoever wins the contest
gets to pay the bill.

'I *insist* on paying,' says Doris
'It's *my* treat!' shrieks mum,
shoving the sweaty £20 note back at her.
'*Please* let me pay,' begs Doris,
scrunching up the note and shoving it
in mum's pocket.
'No, *you* keep your money, Doris,' says mum firmly,
as she prises Doris's shirt open and flicks it down the
    front.
'There now, that's settled!'

Doris jiggles around, vibrating madly,
then untucks her shirt.
The money falls on to the floor.

All the queue is staring
at mum glaring
at Doris glaring
at mum.
You could hear a pin drop
but you can't hear any swearing

and in a fit of daring
I pick up the offending (and now forgotten)
£20 of sterling
and pocket it.

Then mum and Doris burst out laughing
'What a pair we are!' they chorus
as mum gets out her purse
to pay for the tickets.

I feel like a diplomat
on a peace mission
except that I get a hot-dog
in the intermission.
So much excitement
and the film hasn't even begun.
I'm 20 quid richer
and Doris is still speaking to mum.

Animal Rights

Our cat
Won't use the cat-flap
Any more.
He's started to fight
For his Animal Rights
And insists
That he uses the door.

CAT
DOOR
BELL

Dad Can't Dance

A couple of pints of lager
and he's quite red in the face
he thinks he is the business
but he just looks out of place.
He waves his arms around a bit
and wiggles his behind
a more embarrassing spectacle
would be difficult to find.

The Rolling Stones were Number 1
when he last took to the floor
I tell him that the Twist
just isn't trendy any more
(a bit of information
which he chooses to ignore).

But now he's got into the rhythm
the music is loud
he's causing a stir
and he's drawing a crowd.
My friends say: 'Don't worry
he isn't *that* bad!'
It's all right for them
he isn't *their* dad.

He moves like an emu
with three left feet
as a total twerp
he'd be hard to beat

I wish he'd stayed at home tonight
(or at least stayed in his seat).
and if he doesn't take his jacket off
he's going to overheat.

Now he's twitching like a zombie
who's gone into a trance.
He's not too bad at changing plugs
but we shouldn't let him dance!

Typecasting the School Nativity Play

King Herod is played by bossy Ben
The Virgin by simpering Sue
Baby Jesus has gone to dozy Dave –
It was the only part he'd do.

Getting Rid of My Sister

I put my little sister out with the rubbish
and waited for the bin men to come.
But instead of taking her to the rubbish tip
they gave her back to my mum.

Playing Dead

My brother likes to fight with me
and he's usually the winner,
he puts his hands around my throat
to bring up last night's dinner.

He calls me weedy features
as he pulls out half my hair.
He's happier sitting on my chest
than sitting on a chair.

But I have a secret weapon,
a master plan I've devised,
though my brother has seen it a thousand times
it's always a big surprise.

In the middle of a wrestling match
I'll suddenly go quite slack
and act as dead as a dodo,
lying still with my eyes rolled back.

My legs go as stiff as a statue's,
the blood drains away from my face,
and just as my heartbeat grinds to a halt
my brother's begins to race.

What if I'm not just pretending?
How will he tell Mum and Dad?
Who will he torment if I'm not around?
For a sister I'm not quite *that* bad!

He swears that he'll buy me some chocolate,
if only I'll rise from the grave.
So I come back to life and yell 'Gotcha!
Now go get me ten Milky Ways.'

The Boy Whose Imagination
Ran Away with Him

For such a short boy,
Anthony Wriggly told some very tall tales:

Like the one about . . .
His gym shoes being stolen by Martians
His dog, Roger, winning the Grand National
His dad growing up in the only igloo in Rotherham
And his gran having flippers instead of feet.

The teacher warned him:
'Anthony, you must try not to let your imagination
run away with you!'

But one day it did.

It took him to a semi-detached kennel in the middle of
    nowhere
which was owned by a large, and unfriendly, talking
    biscuit.

And then it left him there.

Perfect Paula

Paula is tidy
Paula is good
Paula does everything
nice girls should.

All of the teachers
think Paula is sweet.
But all of our class
know that Paula's a creep.

Perfect Paula's New Year Resolutions List

1. To get everyone hankies for Christmas *and* birthdays because they're nice and useful and you can never have too many (I don't)

2. To be even better at everything than I am already

3. To say lavatory instead of toilet

4. To have the school hamster every holiday and not spoil it

5. To wear cling-film over my nice dress, so as not to soil it

6. To lend people my pencil whilst reminding them gently that if they keep forgetting their own, they'll never be as perfect as I am

7. To write a letter complaining about cruelty to rabbits and bad language on 'Blue Peter'

8. To do long division (just as a hobby) and to show the teacher

9. To say more often: 'Thank you, Mrs Wisley, that was a very interesting lesson, and most educational'

10. To remember to ask: 'Do you mind if I sneeze?' before sneezing, and to reply: 'I'm so blessed already that I'm virtually an angel' if they say 'Bless you'

11. To put my hand up before everyone else. And keep it there

12. To let the world know that chips are bad for you (which is why I never eat them)

13. To tell on the boys who are making puking noises behind my back. Just as soon as I've finished this list.

Grubby Grimethorpe Deals with Dirt

Grubby Grimethorpe
was a big disgrace.
She never cut her horny toenails
or washed her filthy face.
Her bedroom was a cess-pit
which stank of eau de socks.
Was washing up her favourite hobby?
It was *not*.

One day Grubby saw a TV documentary
about a man who never cleaned his flat.
He said that once the dirt got just so deep
it didn't get any deeper than that.

Cleaning, he claimed, was a giant con
for once you started doing it
it just went on and on.

He said that dust and grime
were mostly bits of flaked-off human skin
so it made sense to leave bits of yourself behind
in order to remember where you'd been.

Later Grubby was on her way out
to go mud wrestling
when her mother grabbed her.

'Don't move a mucky muscle,' she yelled,
'you're staying here to help me tidy up.'

'Don't get so worked up, Mum,' said Grubby,
'there's no need to shout.
I've left enough of me behind
to help you out.'

Chuck-it-up Charlie

Charles Unsworth Hegel had a face like an angel
and a stomach as weak as the pound.
When he'd eaten, guess what, he'd chuck up the lot,
he refused to keep anything down.

He threw up over his sister Trish,
he threw up over his cat,
he threw up over his pet goldfish,
as he did it, he jeered, 'Take that!'

When the teacher said: 'Now get in pairs'
no one would be Charlie's partner,
for unless you were sure you were out of his range,
you were dicing with certain disaster.

He had more sick notes than the rest of his class,
which read: 'Charlie's at home feeling bad'.
His talent for puking was unsurpassed,
but it didn't impress his dad.

'I don't think it's clever, this vomiting lark,
and I'm fed up with being ignored.
Your mother's so sick of the puddles you leave
that she won't make your meals any more.'

Charlie grew listless and Charlie grew thin,
there was nothing but bile in his tum,
but he wouldn't abandon his favourite trick
even though it had ceased to be fun.

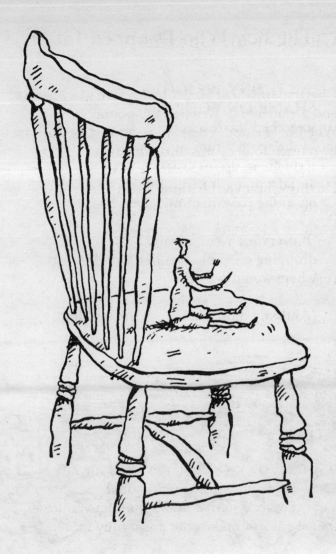

After just a few weeks eating nothing at all,
he had shrunk to the size of an elf.
Charlie's end was unhappy. He soon got so small
that he threw up the whole of himself.

31

The Boy Who Dropped Litter

'ANTHONY WRIGGLY
SHAME ON YOU!'
screeched the teacher
as she spotted him
scrunching up his crisp packet
and dropping it carefully
on to the pavement outside school.

'If everyone went around
dropping crisp packets like you do
where would we be?'

(Anthony didn't know, so she told him)

'We'd be wading waist-high in crisp packets,
that's where!'

Anthony was silent.
He hung his head.

It looked to the teacher
as if he was very sorry.

When in fact he was trying to calculate
just how many packets it would take
to bring Basildon to a complete standstill.

The Boy Who Can't Spell Tries to Look Up Rude Words in the Dictionary

I've tried to look up willee
and lavertoryseets
I've tried to look up botum
but none of them exeests

Read All About It . . .

We've got bingo and pin-ups
with quite pretty faces
we've even got news
tucked amongst the back pages.

Next to pictures of famine
and the starving in pain
we reveal how Fat Fred's
on a diet again.

We've a male politician
found wearing a dress
and an agony auntie
who couldn't care less
and a KEEP BRITAIN TIDY –
NO LITTER campaign
yet we drop all the rubbish we print
in your brain.

We'll ruin someone's life
with gossip and rumour
and when they get upset say
they've got no sense of humour.

We want to sell papers
we want to own minds
we show in full colour
a world that's unkind.
It's a dirty campaign
and we'll know that we've won
when all people believe
what they read in *The Scum*.

Refugee

He can't speak a word of English
But the picture he paints needs no words

In it he puts:

guns
bright orange explosions
a house with no roof
children with no shoes
and his mother and father
lying still, as though asleep.
At the bottom he puts himself, tiny and dark,
with a puddle of blue tears at his feet.
Somehow the fat yellow sun at the top of the page
has a smile on its face.

The Facts of Life

He'll tell you that he slipped and fell
But never that he's gone through Hell
He promised that he wouldn't tell
It's
    just a fact of life

He blocks out the violent threats he hears
And sticks his fingers in his ears
He knows it always ends in tears
It's just
        a fact of life

When things went wrong he cannot say
Feels like it's always been this way
Another bruise, another day
It's just a
          fact of life

Sometimes when things get really grim
He keeps his sweater on in gym
To hide the marks which cover him
It's just a fact
            of life

He stands in the playground on his own
The other kids leave him alone
His misery remains unknown
It's just a fact of
              life

But the teacher notices something's wrong
With the boy who doesn't quite belong
In her office, choking back the tears
He tells of beatings through the years
How life tastes sour like a poisoned pill
The terror which makes him quiet and ill
How he gave up hope and watched it fall
                        Like a dying star
                                    or a punctured
                                                ball

He knows the teacher understands
When she wipes her eyes with her shaking hands
And although she says he's not to blame
He still feels guilty, all the same
Telling the truth is like pulling teeth
Painful,
With more pain underneath
There is no remedy or simple cure
For the nightmare which he must endure

The wounds will take many years to heal
But with help he'll come through the ordeal
Until finally he'll start to feel
He's survived
The facts of life

Just One Day

Mum lost her job and couldn't pay
the rent
so they took our home away.

From a flat
            to the street
took just one day.
Now people rush past
and look away
they think only animals
live this way.

So spare some change or just some time –
Homelessness is not a crime.
I'm a person – my name is Caroline.

Whose Baby?

The spoon misses her mouth
She bangs it on the table in frustration.
She likes to feed herself
And cries if I help her.

I bring her a mirror
I wipe the food off her face.
She watches her life
Going backwards.

She can't walk or crawl
But has already passed her exams,
Been married and read more books
Than I ever could.

Now I read to her at night
And I struggle with words
Which are easy for her mind
But impossible on her lips.

'Good night, Mum,' I whisper.
The crooked smile she returns
Is not at all like a baby's
Though it still says everything she can't.

Why?

Why is just a minute
always several hours?

Why does 'I'll think about it'
always means you won't?

Why are books good for you
and comics bad,
when they've both got words in them?

Why, if oranges are called oranges
because they're orange,
aren't bananas called yellows?

WHY?

WHY?

WHY?

WHY? WHY... WHY!

Why don't they supply batteries
when they sell you a hamster
so that it will have enough energy
to whiz round on its exercise wheel
when your friends visit?

Why does my sister
always cover her spots
with something more noticeable
than the spot is?

Why does my mum always
iron a crease in my jeans?

Why do people always say
'It really suits you'
when you've just had the world's
worst haircut?

And why, if we can go to the moon,
don't we go there more often?

The Loneliness of the
Long-Distance Poet

What's wrong John
Where has all your sparkle gone?
You're like a ping without
a pong
A sing with no song
King without Kong
Kit without Kat
A peg with no leg
A stoat without a coat
Arty without being farty
You're about as much fun
as a funeral party.

And John says:
It's hard to be as happy as a kipper
I've got about as much life in me as a dog-chewed
    slipper
For I've used up all my energy and time
Trying to make this flipping poem rhyme.

I'm Sorry, I've Got a Frog in My Throat

Good evening this is The News.
The Prime Minister announced today . . .

. . . I'm sorry
I've got a frog in my throat,
he's been there for seventeen years.
Sometimes he gets right on my tonsils
and tries to reduce me to tears.

I've told him
I'm sick of his antics
that I think that it's time
that he went.
He makes my breath smell
of pond weed and slime
and he's months overdue with the rent.

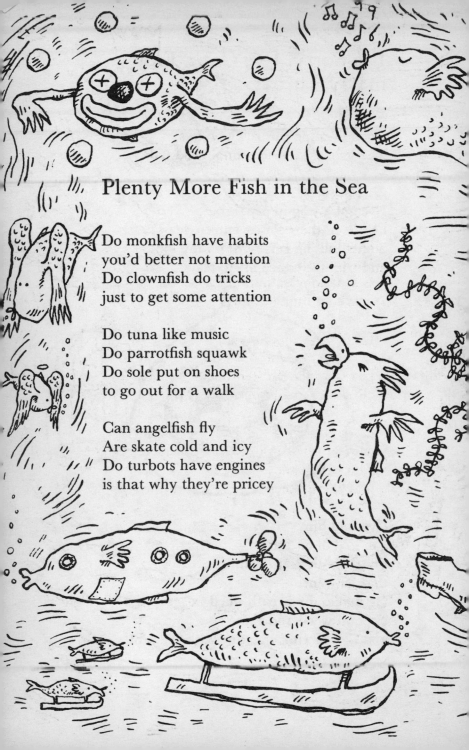

Plenty More Fish in the Sea

Do monkfish have habits
you'd better not mention
Do clownfish do tricks
just to get some attention

Do tuna like music
Do parrotfish squawk
Do sole put on shoes
to go out for a walk

Can angelfish fly
Are skate cold and icy
Do turbots have engines
is that why they're pricey

Do all fish have fingers
Do kingfish wear crowns
Is a haddock a hammock
who's let himself down

Do perch sit like budgies
Do carp mope about
Is a snapper bad-tempered
Do blowfish all pout

Do grouper get lonely
in groups less than three
Don't they know
that there's plenty more fish in the sea?

Derek the Hula Hula Fish

Derek was a Hula Hula fish.
The only Hula Hula
at Arkwright's Exotic Pet Emporium.
The only Hula Hula
in the world
(well virtually).

Derek grew sick and tired of his bowl
he wanted to be a turbot or a lemon sole
to swim out in the ocean with a shoal

Instead of hanging out with a few gerbils
and a clapped-out parrot.

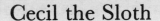

Cecil the Sloth

Cecil's a sloth
he's terribly rude
he yawns in your face
he's got 'Bad Attitude'
He hangs from a tree
with his head pointing south
and a large bit of dribble
hangs
     out
        of
           his
              mouth.

Vince the Confused Alsatian

Vince was meant to be a guard dog:
vicious, mean with lots of nous
But he was completely useless
if you broke into his house.

For Vince thought he was a rabbit
he loved lettuce and his hutch
And though he twitched his nose aggressively
he didn't bark that much

The Boy Who Spoke
Absolute Rubbish

'Flob a lob a lubble lubble
Flob a lob a loo
Flibble, flabble, flobble, flubble
Nee, na na, noo noo.'

'ANTHONY WRIGGLY!'
yelled the teacher
as she spotted him
gibbering into his school bag
instead of answering the question
she'd just asked.
'Sometimes you talk absolute rubbish!'

'It might be rubbish to you,'
said Anthony reasonably
'but it makes perfect sense
to the Grobbit in my bag.'

Little Miss Muffet Fancies a Change

Little Miss Muffet
sits on her tuffet
her temper is starting to flare.
She's angry and mad
'cos her food is so bad
and she thinks that it just isn't fair.
'I sit here all day
forcing down curds and whey
(cottage cheese with some watery stuff)
its taste is as bland
as an old rubber band
and I have had more than enough.

I want burgers and chips
I want ketchup which drips
from the side of my mouth
when I chew
I want bangers and mash
diet Coke, corned-beef hash
shepherd's pie or a prawn vindaloo
I want smooth chocolate spread
slapped all over my bread
a biscuit to dunk in my tea
some barbecued beans
or even stewed greens
to guzzle while watching TV.

Simple Simon has pies
coming out of his eyes
Jack Horner at least gets a plum
and Jack Spratt can eat
lots of lovely lean meat
no wonder I'm feeling so glum!'

Then a spider called Fred
comes and sits on her head
'Stop all this moaning!' he cries
'You're really quite lucky
my diet's much more yucky
for I live on nothing but flies.'

Little Jack Horner (Flyweight)

Little Jack Horner
sits in the corner
is he a boxer or what?
You get this impression
'cos no other profession
sits down in a corner
such a lot.

Humpty Dumpty (The True Story)

Humpty Dumpty
sits on a wall
life as an egg
is beginning to pall,
it's not what it's
cracked up to be at all.

So he jumps.

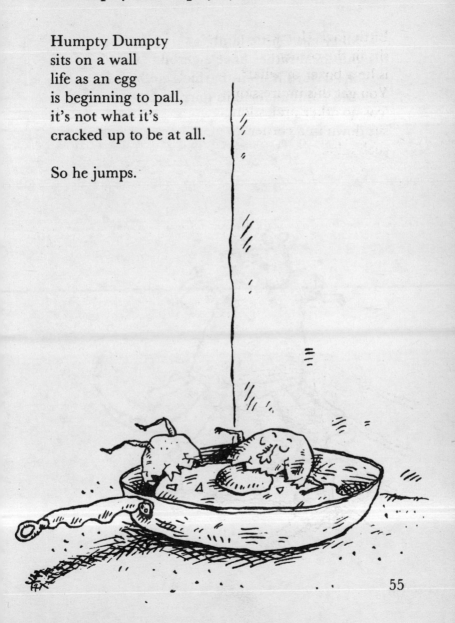

Mary, Mary Quite Contrary

Mary has a little lamb
But she'd rather have a gerbil
She'd dress it up in Barbie's clothes
And paint its toenails purple.

Georgy Porgy Was Not Gorgy

Georgy Porgy
Pudding and pie
Kissed the girls
And made them cry
Here's why —

Georgy was a rubbish kisser
Gob like a frog
And lips like liver
His snogs were wetter
Than a major river
When he went up to girls
And said
'Fancy a snog?'
They'd start to quiver
9 out of 10 girls
Preferred to choose death
Than suffer Georgy's
Foul fishy breath.

Dog Poo Haiku

Smallish brown dog poo
waiting in the street to meet
somebody's flip-flop.

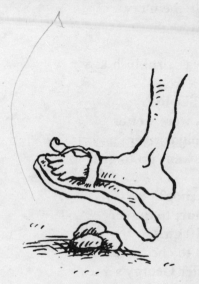

Gnu Haiku

My name makes you laugh
but I *ignu* you
for I am ten times your size.

Kangaroo Haiku

Why do the tourists
always call me Skippy when
my name is Trevor?

Canoc Haiku

I am about as
much use in the desert as
a nylon snow suit.

Angry Loo Haiku

People think it's fun
to pull my handle and quip:
'You look a bit flushed!'

Bored to Death

Anastasia Brough
(pronounced bruff)
Dough-Nought
(pronounced do nowt)
was terribly bored with life.

Hers wasn't just
ordinary common boredom
(perish the thought).
It involved throwing things around
and screeching:
'BORINNGGG!'
so loudly
that whole towns
would have to put in ear plugs.

'Oh Nanny,'
she would wail wearily
for the four millionth time,
'Life's so dull!
Do you think
one could die of boredom?'

'I expect so,'
said Nanny
as she slipped some arsenic
into Anastasia's cocoa.

The Fibber

She calls them bits of fiction
she calls them porky-pies
she calls them super-stories
but she never calls them lies.

The budgie ate her homework
she couldn't believe her eyes,
it made such a mess of his inside bits
that now he never flies.

Her dad's a racing driver.
He races her to school.
He drives at 90 miles per hour
and uses tons of fuel.

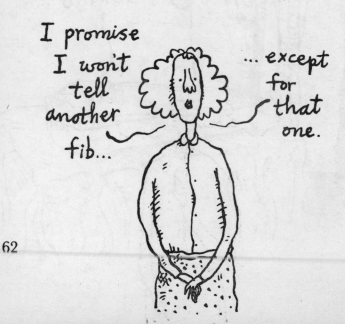

She says that when she's grown up
she wants to be a writer
and get paid to make things up all day,
it's a job which quite excites her.

Or she might go into politics
(after her misspent youth)
or some other nice profession
where they seldom tell the truth.

And on her 60th birthday
when she claims she's 43
those 17 long years
will disappear conveniently.

And when she's finally in her grave
and buried six feet deep,
they'll write on her stone the final fib:

NOT DEAD
BUT JUST ASLEEP

The Boy Who Ate His Sandwiches Too Early While on the School Trip

'ANTHONY WRIGGLY!' boomed the teacher,
'I expect you think you're going
to win an early eater's medal
for having eaten all your sandwiches
by half-past ten. But I am *not* impressed.
Sandwiches are for lunch which is at 1 p.m.'

'But it's already 3.30 in Rawalpindi,' said Anthony,
his mouth full of the final piece of soggy crust.

'But *we* are not *in* Rawalpindi, Anthony,' replied the
    teacher, suppressing a sigh.
'*We* are in Norwich cathedral.'

'Well I'm not *in* that family over there,' said Anthony,
leaping towards a group of complete strangers
and pulling a gruesome face just as they were having
their photo taken,
'but I'll be in their holiday snaps!'

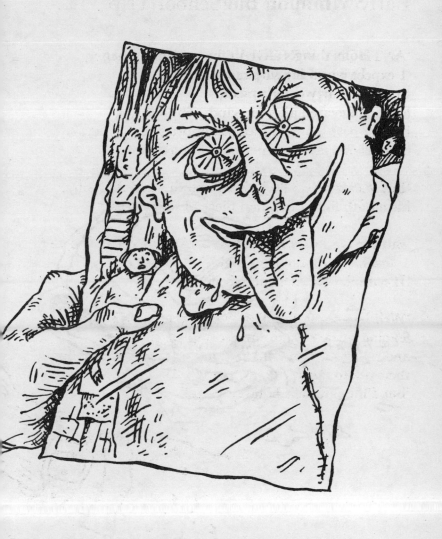

Something's Alive in My Swimming Bag

Something's alive in my swimming bag
I've had my suspicions
And now I'm certain
The emergency services need alerting.

SLITHER...

Egghead

Fred was an eggomaniac
He only ate boiled eggs
He had no heart to make him tick
He had a yoke instead.

A Scab's Complaint

It's hard
being a scab.
You always get picked on.

Rant About Pants

Some people call them knickers
My Granny calls them drawers
Hers used to keep the cold out
Now they're used for cleaning floors

Florists call them bloomers
And lawyers call them briefs
While undertakers solemnly say
A pair of underneaths

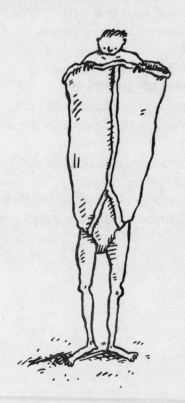

Fire fighters call them hosiery
Americans call them panties
Which are the nasty nylon kind
You get from distant aunties

Small people call them long johns
Tall people call them shorts
There's even combinations
Designed to fit all sorts

Lurking beneath a Scotsman's kilt
You're unlikely to find any
Which makes it nice and easy
When he wants to spend a penny

There are bikinis, teeny-weenies
Trunks with no frills or fuss
You should always wear a fresh pair
In case you're knocked down by a bus

There are hundreds of words for underwear
But I always call mine pants
They're white and clean and seldom seen
And they rhyme so well with ants

I Am a Camera

Whenever Uncle Billy goes away
he takes me along to take some photos.
Yet he cannot make me
take a decent shot,
for he has not got
any talent for photography.

'Smile please,' shouts Uncle Billy
as he points me
at people saying 'cheese'.
He thinks it is a jolly wheeze
but I think that mouthing 'cheese'
never made anyone look cheerful,
it only makes them look teethfull
(and a bit stupid).

Sometimes he wants a close-up
so he shoves my lens up someone's nose
and goes:
'That'll look fantastic!'
but it never does.
It makes them look as though
they've had drastic
plastic surgery
(or a run-in with a large shovel).

And when
the out-of-focus snaps of nasal hair
and people looking cheesier than Camembert
eventually come back,
who gets the flak?
Not Uncle Billy (you can bet on that).
Because he plays by sneaky human rules,
whcrc a shoddy workman *always* blames his tools.

Mrs Wisley's Handbag

I am Mrs Wisley's handbag

She got me at Harrods
I'm made of leather
Wherever she goes
We go together

Once I swung from her shoulder
But now I lie in her lap
'Cos we both are much older
(And she's broken my strap)

Mr Plunkett's Trousers

I am Mr Plunkett's trousers
I do not look quite right
My knees are loose and saggy
While my bottom is too tight.

The zipper in my flies has gone
So staying up's no joke
I'd be happier on a woman
Than this scruffy little bloke.

I wish he'd take me to the mender's
Or just chuck me in the bin
I wouldn't be offended
You should *see* the state I'm in.

I might end up as a patchwork quilt
Spread on a comfy bed
Next to a frock called Marjorie
And a pair of pants called Fred.

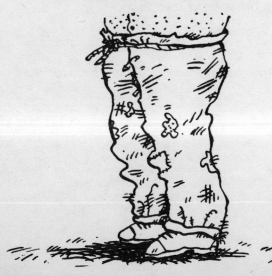

A Luvvy Wins an Award

I'd like to thank my analyst
My agent and my dog
And the handsome personal bodyguard
Who takes me for a jog
Trish who does my make-up
Sue who makes my frocks
And Jean Shamp-oo the hairdresser
Who titivates my locks
I knew I'd tread the boards one day
And eventually be a star
Thanks to all the bores I've trodden on
You all know who you are
I'd like to thank my co-stars
(I suppose I really should)
For although I stole the glory
They did the best they could
Of course I didn't expect to win
(Though I've wanted to for years)
But if they'd given this to someone else
I'd have burst right into tears.

When Anthony Wriggly Was a New Boy

After Assembly
on Anthony Wriggly's first day at school,
the teacher put on her super smile
(the one she only got out for parents
and other trying situations)
and boomed:
'*This*, children, is Anthony.
He is a *New Boy*!'
Then she prodded him,
'What do you say, Anthony?'

Anthony thought about the options
(like 'Hello' or even 'Thank You'),
but instead he said,
'I am not *new* –
I am *five*!'

Down with the Press

They soon got bored with ecology
And filled the paper up with sleaze
And cut the price to 20p
Which really made the sales increase.

Meanwhile . . .
The world ran out of trees.

Life's full of little ironies.

The Punishment

I had a dreadful nightmare
I dreamt I was my dad
I took away my privileges
Because I had been bad.

I sent myself up to my room
And locked myself inside
Then sat there knotted up with guilt
As I broke down and cried.

We were both extremely sorry
But both too proud to speak
So this miserable punishment
Went on another week.

I told myself: 'Give me a break!'
I yelled, 'Give me one too!'
We wound ourselves into a knot
Which no one could undo.

When I woke in the morning
And was myself once more
I thought that sulking half my life
Could start to be a chore.

I made a resolution
I promised to be good
Of course I didn't stick to it
D'you really think I would?

So now when dad is mad with me
I take it on the chin
For though the punishment's hard on me
It's just as hard on him.

Children Also Get Depressed

You say that this month money's tight
That all you ever do is fight
To find the cash when bills are due
You tell me I should think of you
That I am just a nuisance who
Gets on your nerves.

I wonder if you ever guess
That children also get depressed

'Cheer up for God's sake,' you exclaim
You're sorry that I ever came
Into your life ten years ago
'You were an accident you know
We really, truly love you though –
Now tidy your room.'

I wonder if you ever guess
That children also get depressed

You're sick and tired of your lot
You want what someone else has got
Haunted by bitterness and tears
You feel you've wasted all the years
Until you've nothing left but tears
You're wrong you know

I wonder if you ever guess
That children also get depressed

OK so things aren't as you planned
But what I cannot understand
Is why you blame me all the time
It's not as if the fault is mine
The time has come to realize
I see the world half through your eyes
That what you say and what you do
Affects me just as much as you

Although I'm young, my pain's no less
For children also get depressed

2 Poems About 4 Eyes

They call me Specky Four Eyes.
I wear glasses, so it's true,
I can see quite well why you're teasing me,
I've got two more eyes than you.

My spectacles are magical
for when you taunt and jeer,
I only have to take them off
to make you disappear.

Little Red Riding Hood
(The Happy Version)

If Little Red Riding Hood
had worn her specs
it could very well have saved her neck.

For wolves never make passes
at girls who wear glasses.

Hello,
Grandma.

Getting Glasses When You're Older

That life can still be wonderful
I failed to realize
until I had some glasses
fitted to my tired eyes.

Have you
tried contact
lenses,
dearie?

The Richest Poor Man in the Valley

On the outside
he seemed older than he was.
His face was like a weather map
full of bad weather
while inside
his heart was fat with sun.

With his two dogs
he cleared a thin silver path
across the Black Mountain.
And when winter
kicked in
they brought his sheep
down from the top
like sulky clouds.

Harry didn't care for things
that other people prize
like money, houses, bank accounts
and lies.
He was living in a caravan
until the day he died.

But at his funeral
his friends' tears
fell like a thousand
diamonds.

Tales Your Mother Tells You

Crusts make hairs grow on your chest
Sprouts are good for you
And if you suck a biro
Your tongue will go all blue

Mothers tell you lots of tales
Not all of them true

Never eat a bag of chips
You find dropped in the street
There's 20 million billion germs
On every toilet seat
To see another's point of view
You need to use their eyes

Mothers say lots of things
Some of them lies

The longer that you stay in bed
The tireder you get
Gerbils, fish and stick insects
Are unrewarding pets

You'll be bald before you're twenty
If you don't take off your hat
If the wind changes direction
Your face will stay like that
I'll give you £1.50
If only you'll be nice

Mums never call it bribery
They call it sound advice

Solar-powered watches
Are useless in the dark
And as a rule, a dog's bite
Is much worse than its bark
I love all you children equally
But you're all my favourite too
If you want to stop a runny nose
Then don't use super glue

The tales your mother tells you
Seem nonsensical and trite
But when you're old, you'll realize
Your mother's *always* right!

(at least that's what *she* says)

RIPs (Really Implausible People)

Here lie
The ashes
Of Jim 'Houseproud' Groover
Who sucked himself up
With a powerful Hoover

Here lie
The remains
Of 'Fast' Eddy Jakes
Who invented a sports car
Without any brakes

Here lies
The body
Of Annabel Smedley
Who took an eternity pill
Which proved deadly

Here lies
The top half
Of 'Dithering' Freddy
The rest will come soon
When it feels
That it's ready

Anthony Wriggly's School Report

FRENCH (D–)

Anthony has a real talent for languages. Though sadly not one which is spoken on this planet.

Monsieur Le Blag

ENGLISH (B)

Anthony has a lively imagination which might take him further than he thinks one day.

Mrs V. Beastly

GEOGRAPHY (E)

If Anthony paid a little more attention in class, he would know that Eskimos only live in the Arctic Circle. He would also learn that Rotherham is in Yorkshire.

Mr A. Plunkett

HEAD'S COMMENTS

Anthony is not like other boys, nor is he like other girls, which sometimes makes it difficult for him to fit in. He has, however, developed a close relationship with the school gerbil, who is helping Anthony to improve his handwriting.

Mrs Flakey

The Thing About Aardvarks . . .

If you put them in a football team
they wouldn't score a goal
If you took them to a golf course
they'd never find the hole
If they're boxing with a squirrel
they'll come back badly beaten
They cannot win Monopoly
even if they're cheating
If someone let a stink-bomb off

they'd be the last to smell it
If you ask them to write down their name
they'll ask *you* how to spell it.

And even in the 'egg & spoon'
they're bringing up the rear
They never break the finishing tape
to hear a thunderous cheer
And yet there is place
where they are sure of victory
For the aardvark always comes first
in the English dictionary.

Index of First Lines

A couple of pints of lager   19
After Assembly   75
Anastasia Brough   60
'ANTHONY WRIGGLY   32
'ANTHONY WRIGGLY!' boomed the teacher   64
Auntie Doris and my mum   17

Cecil's a sloth   49
Charles Unsworth Hegel had a face like an angel   30
Crusts make hairs grow on your chest   86

Derek was a Hula Hula fish   48
Do monkfish have habits   46

F – fit but not fond of football   12
'Flob a lob a lubble lubble   51
For such a short boy   24
Frank has a dog   13
Fred was an eggomaniac   67
FRENCH (D–)   91

Georgy Porgy   57
Good evening this is The News   45
Grandad is snoring   14
Grubby Grimethorpe   28

He can't speak a word of English   36
He'll tell you that he slipped and fell   37
Here lie   89
Humpty Dumpty   55

I am about as   59
I am Mr Plunkett's trousers   73
I am Mrs Wisley's handbag   72
I had a dreadful nightmare   77
I put my little sister out with the rubbish   21
I'd like to thank my analyst   74
If Little Red Riding Hood   82
If you put them in a football team   92
It's breaktime in the playground   10
It's hard   67
I've tried to look up willee   34

King Herod is played by bossy Ben   21

Little Jack Horner   54
Little Miss Muffet   52

Mary has a little lamb   56
Mum lost her job and couldn't pay   40
My brother likes to fight with me   22
My name makes you laugh   58
My spectacles are magical   81

Oh you canny   9
On the outside   84
Our cat   18
Our dad is addicted to camping   16

Paula is tidy   25
People think it's fun   59

She calls them bits of fiction   62
Smallish brown dog poo   58
Some people call them knickers   68
Something's alive in my swimming bag   66

That life can still be wonderful   83
The spoon misses her mouth   41
They call me Specky Four Eyes   81
They soon got bored with ecology   76
1. To get everyone hankies for Christmas *and*   26

Vince was meant to be a guard dog   50

We've got bingo and pin-ups   34
What's wrong John   44
Whenever Uncle Billy goes away   70
Why do the tourists   59
Why is just a minute   42

You say that this month money's tight   79